WITHDRAWN

Dear Parent:
Your child's love of reading starts here!

Every child learns to read in a different way and at his or her own speed. Some go back and forth between reading levels and read favorite books again and again. Others read through each level in order. You can help your young reader improve and become more confident by encouraging his or her own interests and abilities. From books your child reads with you to the first books he or she reads alone, there are I Can Read Books for every stage of reading:

SHARED READING
Basic language, word repetition, and whimsical illustrations, ideal for sharing with your emergent reader

BEGINNING READING
Short sentences, familiar words, and simple concepts for children eager to read on their own

READING WITH HELP
Engaging stories, longer sentences, and language play for developing readers

READING ALONE
Complex plots, challenging vocabulary, and high-interest topics for the independent reader

I Can Read Books have introduced children to the joy of reading since 1957. Featuring award-winning authors and illustrators and a fabulous cast of beloved characters, I Can Read Books set the standard for beginning readers.

A lifetime of discovery begins with the magical words **"I Can Read!"**

*Visit www.icanread.com for information
on enriching your child's reading experience.*

Library of Congress Control Number: 2018958904
ISBN 978-0-06-289086-3

Cover art by Aleksandar Zolotic
Book design by Erica De Chavez
19 20 21 22 23 LSCC 10 9 8 7 6 5 4 3 2 1   First Edition

I Can Read!

3 READING ALONE

SHAZAM!

BECOMING
SHAZAM

Adapted by Alexandra West
Illustrated by Fabio Laguna
& Walter Carzon Studio

Shazam! created by
C.C. Beck and Bill Parker

HARPER
An Imprint of HarperCollinsPublishers

This is Billy Batson.

He is a foster kid.

Billy's best friend is Freddy.

They go to school together.

Burke and Brett Bryer were the school bullies.

One day, they began to bully Freddy.

They shoved Freddy to the ground.

Billy stood up to the bullies.

But that made them angry.

"Get him!" Burke shouted.

They chased Billy.

Billy ran onto a subway train.

The doors closed behind him just in time.

Burke and Brett clenched their fists.

Billy had gotten away.

Billy let out a sigh of relief.

But then something strange

began to happen.

The lights in the subway train flashed,

and Billy saw strange symbols.

Suddenly, Billy was transported
to a dark cave filled with strange objects.
Something told Billy he wasn't on Earth anymore
He slowly made his way deeper into the cave.
"Is anybody here?" Billy called out.

Billy froze as he saw

an old Wizard sitting on a throne.

The Wizard looked up.

"You are Billy Batson," he said.

"How do you know my name?" Billy replied.

The Wizard struggled to stand as he spoke.

"I am the last of the Council of Wizards . . .

Keeper of the Rock of Eternity."

The Wizard waved his staff.
Billy watched in wonder as a
scene of light came out of it.
"Long ago, there was a battle," the Wizard said.
"The Council of Wizards
fought seven evil creatures."

"We trapped them here," the Wizard continued.

"They've escaped and only a Champion

can trap them again.

You, Billy, have been chosen because you

are pure of heart and strong in spirit.

You are our Champion."

"Now speak my name!" the Wizard shouted.

Billy was in shock.

"But I don't know your name, sir."

The Wizard looked up. "My name is Shazam."

"Wait, for real?" Billy asked.

"Say it!" the Wizard shouted again.

"Okay! Okay!" Billy said.

"I'll say your name."

Billy grabbed the Wizard's staff.

"So, just say it? Like Shazam?"

KRAKOOOM!

The dark cave lit up as lightning
cracked over Billy's head.
Billy's entire body shook
as the Wizard's powers flowed into him.

Billy had transformed into Shazam.

He looked grown up.

He had a red suit and a white cape.

But Shazam was scared.

"Get me out of here!" he cried.

And just like that, Shazam

was back on Earth.

With Freddy's help, Shazam was
able to learn all about his new powers.

He could fly.

He had
super-strength.

He could even create
lightning with his hands!

Even though he was still a kid on the inside, Shazam learned to use his powers for good. Shazam learned to protect the world from bullies, criminals, and magical threats.

Shazam is powerful.

He is Earth's mightiest mortal.

He is a Super Hero.

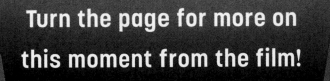

Turn the page for more on this moment from the film!

MEET THE CHARACTERS

BILLY BATSON

A streetwise teenager who is pure of heart and strong in spirit—qualities that led Billy to be chosen to become the adult Super Hero Shazam.

FREDDY

The ultimate fanboy and super hero expert, making him the perfect partner for his new best friend, Billy Batson. He helps Billy figure out his newfound superpowers as Shazam.

BRETT AND BURKE BRYER

The school's toughest bullies, these brothers have a grudge against Billy and Freddy.

THE WIZARD

A mysterious, ancient entity who presides over the Rock of Eternity, protecting its power while also seeking a Champion.

SHAZAM

He's transformed into an adult Super Hero, but inside he's still fourteen-year-old Billy Batson. Despite being in a grown-up, jacked-up body, he uses his newfound powers to become one of Earth's mightiest champions of good.

INSIDE THE ROCK OF ETERNITY

WHAT IS THIS MAGICAL PLACE?

The Rock of Eternity is the physical manifestation of the unique mythology tied to Shazam's backstory. Overseen by the Wizard, it houses the Seven Deadly Sins and the Eye of Sin. It's the stronghold for the magical world—and the source of Shazam's powers.

A MYSTERIOUS FIGURE

The Wizard is weak, but he stands when he sees Billy. Billy is the Wizard's last hope for a Champion.

"SAY MY NAME!"

The Wizard chooses Billy to be the Champion because he is pure of heart and strong in spirit. The Wizard tells Billy to hold his staff and speak his name. His name is Shazam!

THE TRANSFORMATION

Just like that, Billy Batson is transformed into the hero Shazam.

A NEW HERO EMERGES

With the help of his best friend, Freddy, Shazam figures out his newfound superpowers and continues his journey to becoming a real hero.